CHRISTMAS CAROL

A Sweet Christmas Volume 3

SAMANTHA JACOBEY

Lavish
Publishing LLC

First Edition

A Sweet Christmas Series book 3

2017 Lavish Publishing, LLC

All Rights Reserved

Published in the United States by Lavish Publishing, LLC, Midland, TX

Cover Design by: WYCKED INK

Cover Images: ADOBE STOCK

Paperback Edition

ISBN: 9781944985424

www.LavishPublishing.com

Contents

Prologue

GARY GLARED at his computer screen, anxiously chewing the inside of his cheek. Fidgeting with his fingers, he left the device and stood, ambling over to the window to stare at the world outside for several minutes.

"Mr. Ford?" his phone speaker crackled.

"Yes, Agnus," he replied, straightening his tie.

"They're waiting for you in the conference room."

"Oh!" He leapt into action. "I wish you would give me a two-minute warning on these things."

"Yes, sir," she replied, ending the connection.

Collecting his stack of materials, Gary dashed out of his office and raced down the hall. "Sorry I'm late," he mumbled as he took his seat. Glancing around at the others, he tried to clear his head, but lately, he had found being in the office, sitting behind a desk difficult. Paying attention through endless meetings and discussions wore on his nerves in a way he had never imagined anything could.

Two hours later, he made it back from the board-room in time to bid his secretary a pleasant evening. "Are you doing anything tonight?" he asked as she prepared to leave.

"No." She chuckled. "My boys are grown, and there are no grandbabies yet. We'll leave the light on and pass out a few treats, but that's about it."

"Ah, well"—he grinned, waving her off—"enjoy the trick-or-treaters then."

Watching her go, he felt forlorn. He had taken the job as the junior VP in charge of sales when Omar retired in January, to his mother's relief. She had done all that she could to bring him into the family business since he was twenty, and she had finally gotten her wish. He had worked hard and had even enjoyed it on some level through the spring and summer. But as fall set in and the days grew short, he knew he really couldn't hack it.

Oh, he could do the job. He was a good leader and had good people who worked under him. That wasn't the problem. He hated it; that was the problem. The suit, the desk, the stuffy office, and the constant come and go of people. *I can't take it anymore.* He sighed to himself as he packed his briefcase. *I wish I could bring myself to tell Candy I want to go back to the fire department.*

But he couldn't and not just because of his bride. His mother would be devastated if he were to leave after finally agreeing to take the job. Clicking the latches shut, he knew he would have to tough it out. *Maybe things will look better in the new year,* he placated to himself. *Maybe then I'll start to feel...useful.*

Arriving at the house after a stop at the market, Gary pulled into the garage and gathered his briefcase and a couple of blue plastic bags containing a few items for that evening's dinner. Carrying them in, he paused and hit the button mounted on the wall that would close the wide door, hiding his SUV behind it. Turning to the fridge, he stacked his purchases inside, and then called, "Honey, I'm home!" as he placed his black case on the counter.

Bounding down the stairs, his wife of almost a year paused, looking him up and down before she smiled.

"Is something wrong?" he asked, giving himself a quick inspection.

"No," she breathed. "You look so nice. I'm not sure I should wrinkle your suit."

"Don't be silly." He laughed, stepping forward and sweeping her five-foot frame into his arms. "Oh, Candy," he breathed into the top of her hair, the scent of her pushing his worries out of his mind.

"Daddy!" Daks squealed, squeezing in next to his mother to get a grip on one of Gary's legs.

"Hey, buddy!" He patted Dakota on the back, releasing the boy's mother at the same time. "How were things today? Did you have a party at school?" Slipping off his jacket, he followed the younger male into the living room, where his toys were scattered about. Dropping the garment over the back of a chair, he sat on the rug next to the coffee table. "What shall we play?"

"Woo-woos," Daks replied, dragging over the large fire engine Gary had given him two Christmases ago. "Woo-woos, Daddy."

"Woo-woos," Gary repeated, gathering a few items they would need for his stepson's favorite game. "Ok, this is the fire..." he began.

Watching them from the doorway, Candy sighed. Gary had become an excellent father, just as she knew he would. For ten months, their lives had been as close to perfect as anything she had ever known. Her eyes growing misty, she turned her back and dabbed at them, opting for the back porch.

Dammit. She sobbed as she stared at the orange and red painted trees that swayed gently before her.

Everything's going to be fine, she mentally debated. But Candy didn't feel fine. The cooler weather meant that Christmas was coming, and over the years, that holiday had been anything but kind to her.

Her son's special needs and her mother's frailty never far from her thoughts, the young woman wrapped herself tightly with her arms and gave herself a firm squeeze. *Everyone's going to be fine this year*, she repeated her mantra.

Her husband's family would be arriving soon for their traditional Halloween meal, and she needed to finish preparing before they arrived.

Slipping back into the kitchen, she set to work,

focusing on the task at hand. But her mind continued to churn.

After dinner, the children would all set out to trick or treat. *Daks'll enjoy it,* she reminded herself. *And this year, Christmas is going to come and go without a hitch.* At least she hoped that it would.

ONE

Safety First

SIX QUIET WEEKS had passed since the Halloween gathering. On his way to work on a Monday morning, Gary's thoughts drifted back to the event, with all of the cousins gathered in the large ancestral dwelling that he and his new family occupied. And according to tradition, his parents had packed and left for Florida over the following weekend, with him taking them to the airport and bidding them farewell at their departure.

Tapping his fingers on the steering wheel, he gave himself a pep talk, focusing on the positives in his life. Accustomed to their being out of town over the winter, he at least had a family of his own now—a family that brought joy into his once lonely life.

Arriving at the office, his thoughts turned to the holiday season that lay ahead. There was still some debate as to whether his mother and father would return home for Christmas since it normally would be Gary who traveled to see them. However, having

Candy, Dakota, and Lanelle to worry about, he had informed them that they would have to make the trip if they wanted to see him. His mother had taken the news fairly calmly, and he hoped that her seeming to understand was genuine.

Inside the building, Gary pushed the personal issues aside and mentally prepared for his busy day. With a smile, he greeted his secretary warmly. "Good morning, Agnus."

"Good morning, sir," she replied crisply, handing him a few slips of paper containing messages. "Caroline is here to see you," she informed him, indicating the girl seated in the waiting area.

His eyes darting over, he stared at the young woman, surprise flittering across his features. He had been to their attorney's office the previous week, and Ben had introduced him to his new secretary, Diane—the one who had taken Caroline's place when she had mysteriously up and quit her job.

"Good morning," he received the tall blonde politely. "What can I do for you?"

"Hello." Caroline smiled, holding up a manila envelope. "Mr. Monroe needs these documents signed right away if you don't mind."

Gary's eyebrows shot up at her request, but before he could question her, she continued, "It'll only take a moment. I promise. Please." Her lips twitching, he could see the fear in her eyes.

"Sure." He opened the door for her reluctantly. "Come on in." Placing his briefcase on his desk, he turned to face her, then moved to close the portal behind her. "Mind explaining what you're doing here?" he asked in a gruff tone. "Ben told me himself only a few days ago that you had quit."

"I know," she stammered, licking her bright pink lipstick and looking around anxiously, "but I didn't know where else to turn. Gary, I know we have had our hardships and our relationship didn't last that long, but I have always thought of you as a friend."

Pulling off his jacket, he hung it on the coatrack and faced her, arms across his broad chest as he glared at her. "Well, spit it out. I have work to do."

"I can't," her voice squeaked. "Not here. Would you meet me for lunch? Over at Barnaby's."

He squinted at the mention of the bar where they had shared more than a few lunches. Scowling, he couldn't imagine why she would be standing in his office. She was right; she had put him through one of the toughest times of his life, and he considered that even the word *friend* might be stretching the truth a bit. "I'm not sure that's a good idea," he growled, moving past her to sit behind his desk.

Catching his arm, tears formed in her eyes. "Please, Gary. It's not like that!" Her jaw trembled and her words shook. "I need your help. I've gotten into some trouble, and I don't know who to trust."

"So, you came to me." He pulled the arm away, his features softening briefly at the sight of her obvious terror. "What kind of trouble?" he demanded, setting his jaw firmly.

"I'll explain everything at lunch. I'll be there at eleven thirty." Her face morphed into a brief smile as she turned and fled before he could change his mind, not that he had actually agreed to meet her.

Shaking his head, Gary opened his black leather briefcase and removed the documents he had been working on over the weekend. Taking a seat in his chair, he switched on his computer and set to work—a futile effort in light of his former girlfriend's visit. He had known Caroline for a few years and had never seen her that upset—an idea that presented itself frequently to distract him until he was finally able to put on his coat and leave for lunch.

Spying Caroline in a booth along the far wall as he entered, Gary worked his way across the bar. Located downtown, it had been a popular place for businessmen and women to enjoy lunch for almost a century. Taking the cushioned bench across from her, he noticed she wore a dark stocking cap on her head, hiding her hair, and she seemed to be keeping an eye out around her, using frequent covert glances.

"Well?" he asked sharply.

"Thank you for coming," she replied. "As I said, I don't know who else I could trust. I know that Ben thinks I quit my job, but at the time, I didn't really have a choice."

"Did something happen with Ben?" he demanded, noticing the waitress as she approached. "What are you having?"

"Chicken salad on wheat," she replied.

"We'll have two chicken salads on wheat, with ginger ales," he informed the young brunette, who nodded and moved to the next table. When she had gone to get their drinks, he returned to his interrogation. "So, what happened with Ben?"

"I don't know that he's involved," she informed him, pulling the envelope that she had carried earlier out of her over-sized handbag and laying it on the table. "These are for you. Take it with you but don't lose them!"

"What's in it?" He glanced at the parcel, only slightly interested in its contents.

"Over the last two years, I've noticed a few things —unusual things about some of the clients at the firm," she said in a low whisper. "I know you were a fireman. But you were also an investigator, and you have a degree in criminal justice, so I figure you're a good man at heart."

"Thanks." He chortled quietly, somewhat disturbed by her choice words. Seeing his laughter fail to lift her dark countenance, he pushed, "What is it that you suspect?"

"There have been four fires over the last two years," she hissed. "As far as I know, they were all ruled as accidents, but I know for a fact that they weren't."

Anger washed over him, and Gary reached across the table, snatching up the envelope to take a look. Grabbing it back, they fought briefly before he released it to her, realizing they were causing a scene.

"I need to see your proof," he growled.

"You will," she agreed. "When you leave, you can look at it all you want. But I don't think it's safe to take it out here."

Looking around, he wanted to laugh but held his disbelief in check. "Ok, Carol. Let's—"

"It's not Carol," she bit through clenched teeth.

Staring at her, he nodded slightly. "Ok. Caroline, let's start at the beginning. You worked in Ben's law office for about four years."

"That's correct."

"And over the last couple of years, you've noticed some odd…things…about some, or maybe only one, of them."

"That's also correct."

"So, you quit your job and decided to talk to me."

"I quit my job because I was afraid," her voice quavered.

"Fear. Ok." He waved an open palm at her, his trust in her obviously low. "Why?"

"A few weeks ago, someone followed me home. I made it inside, but when I peeked out the window, I could see the guy hanging out across the street where that line of trees is." Her eyes grew wide.

"Do you still live in that apartment?" he asked dubiously.

"Yes. On the third floor," she replied softly. "He was there every time I checked, but I didn't see him when I left for work the next day. That night, when I got home, someone had broken in and had gone through everything—cut the furniture open, flipped over the tables, and pulled out all the drawers. They went through every possible hiding place."

Glancing at the presumed evidence, he shrugged. "They didn't find it?"

"No!" She hit the table softly with her fist. "I didn't hide it at my place! I hid it somewhere no one would think to look. After they broke in, the police came and made a report. They called it vandalism because nothing was stolen. So, the next day, I went into the office, got all my stuff together, and quit. It was the only way I could think of to leave with it and not raise suspicion about it."

Rocking his jaw, Gary recalled how Benjamin had described her departure in just that fashion. *She went in, cleaned out all of her belongings into a few boxes, and informed him that she wouldn't be back.* The hairs on his neck bristled at his first inkling that her suspicions could be valid.

"Who are we talking about? Who did this?" he asked, leaning back against the cushion behind him. "Is Ben involved?"

"I can't tell you that." She sighed. "Not until you agree that you're going to help me."

"Ok." He nodded. "I'm listening. But I need to know more. Who would do this?"

"One of Ben's other clients. Your family are good people, Gary. You work hard, you're honest, you pay your taxes, and you play fair. Not all of the clients at the firm are like that."

"Are you saying that some of Ben's clientele are dishonest?" It seemed naive to him to ever assume that all of them would be upstanding citizens.

"They're more than dishonest," her lips barely moved as she whispered. "They're criminals." She blinked a few times, then continued, "If I'm right, they have burned down or otherwise destroyed at least four buildings, including the one Candy used to live in."

Raising his chin, Caroline now had his full and undivided attention. "You mean they set the fire that Lanelle and Daks nearly died in?"

Hearing the anger in his voice, she knew he was going to help her. "Yes. It was the first one that caught my eye because of your connection to them. After that, the rest only added to my suspicions, and I have a feeling there could be others."

Glancing around, Gary waited. It was a public place, and no one seemed to be interested in the couple. But the idea of accusing someone, anyone, of a felony had him on edge. He wanted to leave, but he could see the waitress approaching with their plates. "Don't say anything else," he cautioned. "Thanks," he offered as the young woman served them while smiling up at her. "Eat," he commanded when she had gone. "I'll take you someplace safe to hide, and we'll discuss this more when I can look at your evidence." Her story seemed incomplete, and although he had become interested in hearing more, he still didn't find her a reliable source.

Not about to argue, Caroline picked up her sandwich and ate at it eagerly. Her appetite had been missing the last few days, but knowing that Gerald Ford was going to help her calmed her nerves, and she suddenly felt like she could have eaten a whole chicken if one had been presented.

As soon as they had finished, Gary dropped two

twenties on the table and escorted the young woman out. Pulling out his cell when they were outside, he made a call to his secretary, informing her that he wasn't feeling well and he would be at home for the rest of the day if anyone needed him.

"What did you do that for?" Caroline demanded curtly. "If they're watching you, you've broken your routine!"

"If they're watching me, that would make them geniuses." He chuckled, squeezing her upper arm and guiding her along. "No one is watching me, at least not yet. If they're following you, which I doubt, then we might have a problem." Reaching the parking garage, he showed her to the elevator and pushed the button to retrieve his ride. "Ok, Carrie, the first—"

"I thought I made myself clear," she snorted, yanking her appendage away. "My name is Caroline. Not Carol, not Carrie, not Lina. Caroline."

Gary stared at her for a moment. "A bit sensitive about that, don't you think? I called you Carrie the entire time that we dated, and you didn't seem to mind then. A nickname is like a show of affection."

"They can be lots of things, and I don't want any part of them."

"Ok, fine, Caroline. We need to locate a shelter for you!"

"A shelter? You mean like a homeless shelter?"

"Maybe." He stepped into the box that had arrived and selected a floor, the idea instantly appealing to him. "Actually, that might not be a bad idea. We need a place no one will think to look, like when you hid the evidence."

"No shelters." The woman crossed her arms defiantly.

"Bah, quit being stubborn. I think it would be a great place to hide. We've got several options. There's the woman's shelter over on—"

"I said NO SHELTER! No half-way house, no group home, no soup kitchen. I wouldn't even consider a cheap motel!" Caroline shouted. "Look, Gary, I need your help, but it's going to be on my terms. There's nothing wrong with my room at the Hilton."

"The Hilton," he spat, exiting the lift and stomping towards his SUV. Glancing at her, he recalled how she had always had a taste for high living—the one attribute that had brought their relationship to a sordid and painful end.

Studying her, he could feel his star witness in whatever had transpired in all those fires disappearing as soon as his back was turned, and he couldn't let that happen. *I have to get her to stay somewhere I can locate her when I need her, but anyone after her can't get to her.* "How about a cell downtown?" he teased.

Her eyes wide, her shocked expression took the wind out of his laugh.

"Hey, I was only kidding!" He stepped towards her to catch her arm, as she suddenly appeared to be a scared animal ready to bolt. "Caroline, calm down. Everything's going to be fine, and I know just the place. We'll go get your stuff, and I'll take you home with me."

"Home with you!" she gasped. "Listen here, *Gary*," she bit his name as if it were a curse. "Of all the wrong places, home with you has to be the worst idea of all!"

Blinking, he grimaced, fairly certain that his wife was going to agree. "Well, I think the Hilton, or any other hotel, isn't any better. If someone is looking for you, that's the first place they'll go." Opening the door for her, he waited for her to climb inside and then strutted around to the driver's side.

"I'm not going to argue with you about this. We'll go to the hotel and get your stuff. But don't check out. I'm taking you home with me, and that's final."

"Why should I not check out?"

"Don't worry about that part." He grinned deviously. "We can use the Hilton as a decoy. If they find out you're booked there, whoever it is we're dealing with might waste a few days camped out there waiting for you."

"Do you really think they're looking for me? I thought leaving my house would be good enough. I couldn't stay there, the way they trashed it, you know." Her voice trailed away, filled with sadness.

"I know," he agreed, patting her leg. Pulling up in front of the large building, he looked around for any cars that might have been following them. Not seeing anything identifiable, he stated confidently, "I think we're in the clear, at least for now. Let's go so we can get out of here."

Fifteen minutes later, her suitcase had been packed. Hanging the "do not disturb" sign on the knob on his way out, Gary grinned at his ploy, sure that keeping the maids out would help hide the fact that she had abandoned the suite.

TWO

Shady at Best

BENJAMIN MONROE SHIFTED stacks of papers, searching for his phone. His desk cluttered, his life had fallen into utter chaos in a matter of days. Rubbing his face roughly with his right hand, he clenched the left into a tight fist, then slammed it down on the mess before him. *I have to do something, but what?* He was in deep, and the odds of getting out were mounting against him.

Locating the device, he lifted the receiver and made the call. "Yes. Gerald Ford, please." Listening to faint music, he waited. "Hello? Yes, I need to speak to Gary, please."

"I'm sorry, but Mr. Ford is out for the afternoon," Agnus explained over the line.

"Oh," Ben gasped, slapped by the news. "Will he be in tomorrow?"

"I'm afraid I can't say," the older woman replied. "He wasn't feeling well, so maybe tomorrow, but I'm not sure."

"Ok, I'll try back in the morning," Ben agreed, ending the connection and dropping the phone into the cradle. Pushing back from his desk, he picked up his coat and slid his arms in while exiting the inner office. Pausing to speak to the young woman seated in front of the portal, he smoothed his hair and straightened his tie.

"Can you get me Gerald Ford's home address?" he asked in as casual a tone as he could muster.

"Yes, sir," his new receptionist, Diane, replied with a smile. Printing the page, she presented it to her boss. "Would you like to set up an appointment with him?"

"No," Ben clipped, studying the information. "I gave him a call, but he's out for the afternoon."

Looking up at her employer, the young woman had only held her position a few days, and she had her doubts about certain things. She felt confident interrogating her benefactor about his intentions would be crossing the line, so she left it at that and returned to her work. Ignoring her, Ben walked slowly towards the front door and out to the street while folding the page in half a few times and tucking it inside an inner pocket.

At his vehicle, the middle-aged attorney slid behind the wheel of his shiny, black BMW. His mind turning his options, he felt sick—sick of the mess he had created for himself. *Will dragging Gary Ford into this do any good?* he quibbled mentally. *He isn't part of the community at the city offices any longer.* But the man had the knowledge and skills that could save Ben's ass if anyone could.

Making the necessary turns, he arrived on a narrow street half an hour later. Rolling slowly past the large, stately structure that had been in the Ford family for generations, he glared at it as if he could see through the walls. Diverting his attention back to the road, his heart leapt into his throat as Gary's SUV glided past with Caroline Baker seated in the passenger seat. "What the hell?" he muttered out loud. Pulling over to park against the curb, he grabbed the rear-view mirror and twisted it to watch the vehicle turn into the familiar drive and disappear. Blinking a few times as if the scene would change, his breaths came in quick, shallow pants.

"Caroline knows," he mumbled. "She has to. That's why she quit all of a sudden." But how, he couldn't be certain. He had only caught on that something wasn't right a few days ago, and his former secretary had already pulled her little disappearing act. "Maybe she's working for them," he surmised aloud.

Moving up the street, Ben swung the car around and parked facing his target. He couldn't knock on the door not knowing why Gary and Caroline were together, but he could wait for a chance to get the other man alone and confront him. Either way, there wouldn't be any point in going back to the office until he had done a bit of hardcore thinking about a few of his clients—the ones he knew were shady at best and most likely to kill him just to shut him up.

Laying the seat back a bit, Ben leaned against his arm and closed his eyes. Slowly, he replayed the discovery he had made only four days ago—the discovery that had meant his life would never be the same. He had always suspected that some of his clients were not on the up and up, but he had never intentionally helped anyone commit or even cover up a crime.

Intentionally. He scoffed at the word. *Fat lot of good it does me now.* He had been helping one of his clients last week with filing some paperwork—claims about a fire that had destroyed one of his buildings. That in itself wasn't unusual. There had been several such instances over the years, and dealing with such unfortunate tasks were part of the job.

Shuddering, he recalled the instant the name on the official report sank in. *Harvey Waters.* He had seen the name before. Pushing the recognition aside, he had finished the filing and had the case completed. For all practical purposes, the matter had been settled on Thursday, but on Friday, he couldn't stop thinking about it.

That's when he started digging. Locating three other cases he had filed, all involving fires over the last two years, he had found the name Harvey Waters attached to all of them. *Son of a bitch.*

Opening his eyes, Ben stared down the road in the fading light. "This isn't getting me anywhere," he mumbled, sitting up straight in his seat and biting his knuckle for a moment. "I should just suck it up and go down there. Hell, it'd be better than sitting here waiting."

Half an hour later, he cranked the engine and eased down the road, making the turn into the private drive and cutting off the lights as he parked behind Gary's ancient house.

THREE

Looking for a Home

"WOULD you like to explain to me what the hell is going on?" Candy demanded, her voice barely short of an angry shout.

"What do you mean?" Gary blinked at her. "We have plenty of room. Caroline hit a rough patch in her life. She needs a job and a place to stay. We need someone to help with your mom and Daks. It's a win-win situation!"

"That's not what this is, Gary! This is just another instance of you bringing home another stray! When someone is looking for a home, it doesn't mean *you* have to help them find it!"

"Come on, honey! This is Caroline. She was Ben's secretary, and I've known her for years," he cooed, skipping the darker parts about her being an ex-girlfriend or what she had done to him.

"If she worked for Benjamin Monroe, why does she need a job now? Did he fire her?" Candy asked crossly, her arms folded tightly in front of her.

"I'm not sure what happened to be honest," he lied flatly. He had known his wife would be a tough sell, but he had underestimated her. "All I know is she's lost her apartment, her job, and she could use a place to stay and a steady income. With Christmas coming, you know you're going to need the extra pair of hands."

Glaring at him, Candy's chest heaved. Grinding her teeth, she had to admit he had a point, at least in that regard. "If I agree to this, you have to promise me that it's only temporary."

"Absolutely." He raised his right hand as if taking an oath.

"And if we have any trouble at all, she's out!"

"Yes," he agreed, his head bobbing around in an odd circle.

"All right. Then she can have the bedroom I stayed in before we were married. Maybe we should move Daks to the one across the hall from her. I'd rather he shared our bathroom than hers," she pondered aloud, "and I'm certainly not sharing ours with her."

"They'll be fine. It's a lavatory, and they won't be using it at the same time." He grinned, happy she had finally agreed. "I don't think uprooting him will be necessary, and I understand your wanting to keep ours to yourself."

Downstairs, Caroline sat on the edge of a chair, wringing her hands as she watched Dakota play with his toys in the middle of the large living room floor. Above them, she could hear the muffled voices as

Gary and Candy worked out their disagreement, causing her frazzled nerves to grow tense to the point of cracking.

"Would you like a drink?" Lanelle interrupted her thoughts.

"Tea…if you have it." The younger woman forced a smile. Standing, she followed the slouched form into the kitchen. She didn't know much about Candy and her mother, only that the elder had survived a stroke, which had made life difficult for her. Then, she had been trapped in the mysterious fire that had occurred two years ago, leaving Candy's mother completely at the mercy of others.

Watching as the trembling digits unwrapped the bag and placed it in a cup of hot water, she smiled in earnest. "Thank you," she breathed, accepting the saucer and matching cup. "Should we return to the front room?" She indicated the young man through the wall.

"I can see him," Lanelle replied, placing her own beverage on the table at her favorite seat. From there, she could watch into the other room without hanging over the boy. "I like to give him a little space." She grinned.

"But not too much," Caroline agreed.

"Yeah." Lanelle nodded, sipping her warm drink. "So, Gary wants to hire you to help take care of us. Do you have much experience with frail old women and difficult children?"

Caroline gasped at her choice of words.

"It's ok." Lanelle laughed in a gravelly voice. "I

know we are more than a handful for Candy these days. I see the tired in her eyes. It's good of my son-in-law to find her some help."

Caroline pursed her pink lips, swallowing hard as she formulated her reply. "I've had a bit of experience." She exaggerated her few babysitting adventures as a teenager, unsure if the old woman had recognized her from the single time they had met. Finally deciding the truth, as far as she could take it, would suffice, she asked in a quiet monotone, "You don't remember me, do you?"

"You've got a familiar face." Lanelle shook her greying locks. "But I can't place you. My mind's grown fuzzy over the years with all the things clogging it up." She smiled, exposing a few crooked teeth and revealing the abuse her body had endured.

"I'm Caroline Baker," her companion stated firmly. "We met at Ben Monroe's office last year. I was his secretary, but I've had to leave under unfortunate circumstances." She paused, watching the wrinkled expression as clarity settled in, and she smiled. "I'm glad I'll be able to help you."

"Yes." Lanelle gave her another toothy grin. "We're glad you are, too!"

Unsure of her sincerity, Caroline did her best to return the smile. Sipping her drink, she waited for the couple arguing above them to come down and give them the verdict. When the wait grew long, she filled the air with small talk, and the older woman opened up about Candy and Gary's relationship, spilling a few of the details of the couple's courtship and wedding.

When she had heard enough, Caroline offered, "Well, it looks like we'll need to make dinner soon. Is there something I can do to help?"

"We've got a lasagna in the freezer," Lanelle offered, "and we can put together a salad from the vegetables in the fridge."

Rising, Caroline didn't hesitate to take charge of preparing the meal. Setting the oven to preheat, she gathered the ingredients for the side dishes. Spying the bread on the counter, she set up the toaster oven to warm a few slices when everything else had fallen into place.

An hour later, Gary and Candy joined them at the table as the meal was served. "Everything looks great!" the mistress of the house observed, her features doing little to hide her displeasure at the situation.

"Thanks," Caroline replied in a warbled voice. "I'm sorry about my intrusion. I know you weren't expecting me like this."

Studying the two women, Gary considered his choice to keep his bride in the dark about their guest's true circumstances. In the end, knowing why she had joined them would only make her worry. Right now, Candy didn't need that, and he knew it. Seeing his wife smile, he exhaled a loud sigh of relief. "Thanks for making dinner. It looks great," he complimented firmly.

"That's going to be my job, isn't it?" the blonde

perked up, her enthusiasm genuine. "I'll be in charge of taking care of the house, looking after Lanelle and Daks." She indicated the pair with a wave of her hand. "All of those things, right?"

"Yeah," Candy agreed, her heart still not in it. "I'm busy with my classes, so I do appreciate the help."

"Well then." Caroline motioned at their seats. "Shall we?"

Settling in for the meal, the conversation came in small spurts as the group adjusted to their newest member. That is until a pair of headlights lit up the back yard as a car pulled into the parking area behind the house and shut off its engine.

Gary made it to the window first and peered into the darkness. Seeing Ben climb out of the black sedan, his heart pounded noisily in his ears. "Damn. I have to take this," he muttered, passing off the arrival as business-related. "You go on and enjoy the meal, and I'll be back in a minute," he commanded as he shoved his arms into his jacket and exited via the back door.

FOUR

Thug Life
_____

STOMPING across the wooden planks of the back porch, Gary raised his hand and called, "What're you doing here?"

Shrugging, Ben felt a sense of relief that there would be no beating around the bush. "I need to speak to you…in private."

Bewildered for a moment, Gary wasn't sure what to make of the older man's arrival or his casual demeanor.

"Take up a chair," he offered, wafting a hand at the picnic table, which was clear at the moment but would be covered with snow most of the winter.

"Thanks. I'll stand," Ben replied, shoving his hands in his pockets as he ambled away from the house and farther into the yard. "I guess you know we've got a bit of a situation here."

"Yes, I know," Gary replied, taken by the sudden urge to pull out a cigarette and light it up. He had quit when Candy and Daks had first moved in with him and, for the most part, never gave them a second thought. But the stress of that particular Monday had sent the craving coursing through him. "Is it safe to talk here?" he asked in a quieter tone.

"As safe as anywhere, I guess." Ben chuckled, then ran his fingers through his silver-streaked hair. "I wish I could spill everything I know, but that would be against attorney-client privilege."

"Then what are you doing here?" Gary repeated.

"I need your help," Benjamin confessed. "Their privilege ends when I feel my own life is in danger. I don't care what the rules say."

"If your life is in danger, why haven't you gone to the police?" Gary demanded, his face growing flushed.

"There's some things even the police can't help with," Ben mused. "When you live a thug life, you sometimes exist outside the law."

Gary curled his tongue, considering the other man's choice of words. "You consider yourself a thug?" He had never thought of Benjamin Monroe as even remotely crooked, much less a full-fledged criminal.

"No, not in so many words." Ben grinned sheepishly. "But some of my clients probably wouldn't hesitate to settle this in a most unpleasant fashion if they thought I was going to reveal anything crucial about them."

"I see." Gary nodded, wondering if Ben knew about Caroline's being there or her suspicions. "How deep are you into this?"

"All the way." Benjamin laughed out loud, cutting his eyes up to stare into Gary's deep brown orbs. "I swear I didn't have a clue what was going on until last week. I was filing the last report, and it hit me like a ton of bricks."

"Last week," Gary agreed. "Caroline had already quit by then," he offered.

"Yes, she was already out of the office. I went digging on my own, and I think I figured out why she took off in such a hurry."

"She's scared, Ben."

"So am I. These aren't street hoods, the guys who did this. They're real professionals."

"You have proof of that?" Gary growled, shifting his weight from one foot to the other.

"I could follow the paper trail well enough. What gets me is that the four I pieced together were all in my office. My clients. What if there's others? How big could this thing be? Worth more than my life to someone, I'm sure. All our lives, in fact."

Gary stiffened, shifting his gaze to the lighted window, where his family sat enjoying their dinner. Fear tightened his gut, and he asked in a husky tone, "Would they have followed you here?"

"I doubt it." Ben shook his head. "They don't know that I'm on to them. I haven't met with anyone else. If we move quietly, maybe we can get to the bottom of this. Get the proof we would need to make sure they go to jail and they don't come out."

"Lawyers don't normally talk about sending their own clients to jail," Gary sneered.

"Like I said"—Ben stretched to his full height —"their privilege ends when my life is in danger. If they set those fires, they have blood on their hands. I'm a financial attorney, and I didn't hire on to protect them from the law when it comes to murder."

Nodding, Gary agreed. "All right then. Go on about your business, and I'll be in touch tomorrow, Wednesday at the latest. Right now, I have to figure out what I'm going to tell Candy."

"She doesn't know?"

"No. And I want to keep it that way. If she ever thought I might have put her in danger by bringing Caroline here, she would never forgive me. I just hope that's not what I've done."

FIVE

Isn't That Sweet

LICKING HER LIPS, Caroline pushed the food around on her plate. She had been hungry when they first sat down, but the arrival of the unannounced visitor outside had stolen her appetite away.

Watching the other woman fidget, Candy herself grew uneasy. "I'm sure it's someone from the office," she reassured. "This isn't the first back-porch meeting that Gary has had since he started working at his family's business." She grinned.

"They stop by often?" Caroline tried to sound upbeat.

"Yeah. They're related, so they don't see any harm in blending home and work. All one big happy family," Candice breathed.

"Gary's family has been very good to us," Lanelle interrupted, indicating the back door with her fork.

"That's true." Candy nodded, then reached over to help Daks by chopping up his lasagna better. "I'm not complaining."

"That's sweet," Caroline muttered, thinking about her previous dealings with the Ford clan. She had made a young and foolish mistake with Gary, one that had come to trouble her deeply over the years.

Caroline had been working for Benjamin Monroe for about six months when Gary had first asked her out. Instantly taken with the idea of hanging on his arm and being part of his luxurious life, she had eagerly accepted, and their relationship had turned physical in a matter of days.

Of course, the party had been over after only a few weeks, and it would have ended there if she hadn't refused to let him go so easily.

Rather than bow out gracefully, Caroline had tried to force Gary to continue seeing her. Informing him that she was pregnant had held them together for an additional couple of months, and she had tried vigorously to conceive during that time. In the end, she had been unable to accomplish her goal, and he had broken things off for good when he discovered the truth about her condition.

Things had been strained between Gary and herself ever since. If Eve held a grudge, it didn't show, but Caroline could feel the cold vibe any time that Gerald or his father were in the same room.

She sighed at the recollection of how things had turned out, and a moment of regret at having asked him for help washed over her.

"Are you ok?" Candy interrupted her thoughts.

"I'm fine," Caroline lied. "It's been a rough few weeks. I just need some rest."

"Let me show you to your room," Candy offered, getting to her feet. "Mom can take care of washing Daks up, and I'll polish off the dishes when I come back down."

Picking up her suitcase from the living room where she had left it, Caroline followed the lady of the house up the stairs to the first bedroom at the top of the stairs. Inside, she looked around at the simple décor. "It's nice," she offered, placing her bag on the foot of the bed.

"The bathroom is in here." Candy opened the portal to indicate the lavatory. "Dakota's room is on the other side, so you may want to lock his door when you use it. Wouldn't want him giving you any surprises." She giggled.

"No, we wouldn't. I'll be sure to do that," Caroline agreed while opening her pack and sorting through her things nervously. "I wanted to thank you, Candy. I appreciate you letting me stay here and for giving me a job."

Smiling in earnest for the first time since her arrival, the shorter girl nodded. "I'm glad you're here. I know I made a fuss, but I really could use the help."

"You're going to school, right?"

"Yeah. This is my third semester, and I'm still trying to get a straight-A report card!"

"What are you taking?" Caroline relaxed, pulling out a few items and selecting a drawer to place them in.

"I want to be a physical therapist." Candy

beamed. "I'm knee-deep in basics right now, but soon I'll be able to apply to some programs."

"Did you choose that because of Dakota?"

Her smile lessened, Candy paused, unsure of how to respond. "I guess I did," she confessed. "He's a special child. He has needs that make him unique." She swallowed hard, not wanting to delve into how her own shortcomings had led to his birth and his unfortunate condition. "It's not something I'm ready to share with you," she stated calmly.

"I understand." Caroline smiled, looking over at her new friend. "We all have things in our past that we don't like to talk about—things that we've done or that have happened to us. Life isn't always…sweet."

Candy nodded slowly, confident that their new caregiver understood. Hearing the back door close below, she grinned. "I'll leave you to your unpacking. Have a warm bath and get some sleep, and I'll fill you in on our routine in the morning."

"Yes, ma'am." Caroline gave her a small wave as Candy closed the door.

Clomping down the stairs, she arrived to find that her mother had removed the boy and had him in the bathtub in her quarters off of the kitchen. Listening to the pair of them for a moment at the door, she sighed. They both seemed unaffected by the arrival of Caroline, which could be a good thing.

Gary sat at the table, watching his wife while he ate. "Did you get her settled in?"

"Yeah. She's in my old room. I guess she's going

to be ok. Daks seems to like her well enough. I know Mom does."

"Of course they do," he chortled, folding his hands. "She's going to be a great nanny."

"Yup," Candy agreed, taking plates and scraping the scraps into the trash before placing them in the dishwasher. "This year, we're going to have a quiet, uneventful Christmas."

Gulping down a few swigs of tea between bites, Gary hoped his wife was right about that, but if his conversation with Ben had been any indication, they were in for one hell of a ride.

SIX

Not What You Think

THE FOLLOWING MORNING, Gary cornered Caroline in her bedroom before she could go downstairs. "I need to take your envelope to the office with me," he demanded in a hushed tone.

"Why?" she gasped.

"I haven't seen your evidence yet, and I want to have a look at it."

"Then come in and close the door. I'll show you what I've got!"

Stepping back into the hall, Gary glared at her. Going into her new room and closing the door would be out of the question for more reasons than he could count. "No, thanks." He raked the air with his hand as if swiping the idea of it away. "Give it to me, and I'll look when I get to work."

Her mouth twisted into an angry pucker, Caroline retrieved and handed over her bundle. "Promise me nothing will happen to it," she hissed.

"I swear it will be perfectly safe. I'll make copies

of anything I need and bring the originals back to you tonight," he offered, palming the pack and turning away. Placing it in his briefcase in his office on the first floor a moment later, he breathed a sigh of relief. He hated the idea of deceiving Candy, but for the time being, the less she knew the better. Hearing the morning chatter in the other room stirred feelings of guilt within him, and he would be hard-pressed to keep the secret for long.

Joining the others in the kitchen, he discovered that Caroline had come down directly after him and had taken over the cooking. Frying scrambled eggs on the stove, she didn't even look up when he entered.

"Daddy!" Dakota squealed, reaching for a hug with jelly-coated fingers.

"Hey, buddy!" Gary replied. "Don't smear the suit, ok?" he teased as he moved in for a quick squeeze.

It had taken months for Dakota to learn to keep his hands to himself when they were dirty, but they had managed to impart at least that portion of wisdom to him. Watching the pair, Candy smiled with pride. If there was anything odd in Gary's behavior, she didn't seem to notice, and he made his escape half an hour later, headed to work and a safe place to go over whatever it was that had both Ben and Caroline afraid for their lives.

As soon as he had gone, Candy sat down and wrote out their daily schedule. "This is the usual around here, but we get doctor appointments and other interruptions pretty regular," she informed the blonde as she handed her the list.

"Looks simple enough," Caroline agreed, studying the page and noting Candy's cell number at the top. "I'll get him off to school and then give the house a deep cleaning, starting with the kitchen here."

"A deep cleaning?" Candy sounded miffed.

"Well, sure!" Caroline grinned. "With as busy as you've been, I'm sure it could use an extra scrub!" Seeing the anger simmering in her employer's hazel orbs, she backtracked. "It's not what you think. I don't mean that your house is dirty. On the contrary, it's probably as clean as you and Lanelle can keep it. But I'm here to help take it to the next level, so please don't be offended!"

"Who says I'm offended?" Candy shot back coolly, reaching for a rag to give Daks a quick wipe before leading him up to a proper bath. Scrubbed and dressed, she returned with him a few minutes later to discover the other woman had already begun the process and had cleared the countertops to do the job justice.

"I'll be back late today. This is my Tuesday–Thursday class, and we have a lab," Candy stated crisply.

"No worries," Caroline reassured. "Dinner will be ready when you get home."

"Don't wait for me," Candy insisted. "Feed everyone else, and I'll warm up a plate when I'm ready." Not looking at her as she spoke, she fought actual tears as they slipped into their jackets and went out to wait for Dakota's bus at the end of the drive.

"Do you think I've upset her?" Caroline asked Lanelle, who sat at the table, enjoying her coffee as the discussion had unfolded.

"Not really." Lanelle grinned over the rim of her cup. "My daughter is very stubborn. She doesn't like to need or accept help. Don't worry. She'll get over it. Just give her time."

Caroline nodded, feeling oddly disturbed by Candy's displeasure. Attacking the grime she had discovered beneath the canisters that had lined the back of the laminate tops with vigor, she thought about the time she had spent with Gary before Candy came along. In truth, she had hurt him very deeply with her ploy to trap him into a permanent relationship.

Perhaps her taking care of his wife and home could be her way of making it up to him. Besides, if he helped her solve the mysterious fires by bringing those responsible to justice, then she would owe him an even greater debt for getting her out of an impossible situation.

Once she had finished the scrubbing, she cleaned out the fridge and freezer, removing spills and moldy leftovers.

Watching her all the while, Lanelle smiled each time she squealed at some new, gruesome discovery. "I dare say it's been months since Candy had time to do any of that," the older woman finally informed her.

"I can tell," Caroline agreed, plunking down in a

chair with a cup of hot tea for a break. "This is much different than being a secretary. That's for sure," she whined as she inspected her manicure.

At that moment, the phone on the wall rang, causing them both to jump. Staring at each other for a moment, Lanelle finally stood, since it was mounted almost directly over her head, and lifted the receiver. "Hello?" her voice grated into the mouthpiece. When no one replied, she tried again, "Hello? Is anyone there?" to no avail. Hanging up the handset, she shrugged. "Usually, it's someone selling something. Oh well." Shuffling into her bedroom, she called over her shoulder, "If you don't mind, I'm going to lie down for a bit. Wake me when lunch is ready?"

"Yes, ma'am," Caroline called after her, disturbed by the mysterious call. Making her way to the front room, she peered out through the curtains at the long private drive and front yard. Seeing nothing out of the ordinary, she closed the drapes and returned to her chores to keep herself occupied until time to prepare the next meal.

SEVEN

Who Do You Trust

GARY HAD a sales meeting as soon as he got to the office, so it was close to lunch before he could open his briefcase and bring out the incriminating files. His chest tight with apprehension as he opened the bundle, he spread them out on his desk and looked over them one by one.

Each was a packet of documents about a fire, including a copy of the insurance policy and who was paid for the losses. The beneficiaries had been different, and Gary began to wonder if Caroline's perceived connection had been some sort of game she wanted to play with him. He couldn't put it past her based on her previous performance.

Flipping through the pages, he noticed that each also contained an official investigation report from downtown. An investigator had signed off on them in turn, declaring them to have been accidents. When he reached the third stack, he did a double take and had to look back at the others to be sure. *Yup. All signed by Harvey Waters.*

That in itself would not have seemed odd if Harvey had been the only investigator the city had, but as one of three, the fact that his name appeared on all four caused a quiet alarm bell to ring in Gary's mind. Couple that all four of the victims were clients of Ben Monroe, and all had their buildings burn to the ground in such a close time frame...

A shiver ran up Gary's spine at the recollection of the fire that had come near taking his mother-in-law and stepson's lives two years ago. "These were no accident," he mumbled aloud, flipping the rest of the pages, hoping to find some other clue.

Unable to locate anything else, he decided to start there. But first, he needed to arrange a meeting with the only people he felt he could trust at that exact moment—Caroline Baker and Benjamin Monroe. But how? He couldn't have Caroline roaming around in public if someone was after her. They would have to be discreet.

Snapping his fingers, he recalled that being Tuesday, it would be late in the evening before Candy arrived home. "If I plan this right, we'll be done and Ben will be gone before she gets there." Of course, Lanelle would know about the meeting, so he would have to work around that, but an excuse would be easy to manufacture.

Deciding he would have to risk it, he made the quick call to Ben's office, but Diane informed him that he was in court. "Well, shoot. Could you let him know that Gary Ford called?"

Recognizing the name, Diane laughed. "Mr. Ford! Ben was trying to reach you yesterday! I guess the two of you keep missing each other. He even took your address when he left, so I assumed he went to see you at home."

"No." Gary hesitated, then had an idea. "I guess he changed his mind. But if you can get a message to him, tell him to come over for dinner tonight. We'll talk then," he added with a jovial chuckle for effect.

"I'll text him exactly that," the receptionist agreed before hanging up.

Deciding to give Caroline a heads up, Gary next dialed the house, which his target answered on the second ring.

"Hello, Ford residence!"

"Caroline, it's me, Gary. Are you ok? You sound flustered."

"I'm fine," she replied breathily. "I'm cleaning. What do you want?"

"I've invited someone over for dinner, so make an extra serving," he informed her crisply, considering for a moment if he should keep their guest's name to himself. Deciding it might be better if she was prepared, he continued, "It's Ben."

"Ben! Are you crazy?" she hissed. "I told you I think he might be involved—"

"He's not involved," Gary soothed, cutting her off. "He's just as scared as you are. He's the one who came to the house last night, and I think you're both right about things being questionable with these incidences."

"Well, I'm glad you agree." She huffed in his ear.

"Yes. But I really don't want to drag Candy into this if we can help it. So, dinner needs to be ready so we can eat, talk, and get him out of there before she gets home."

"Ok. I'll take care of the dinner part," Caroline reluctantly agreed. "What about Lanelle?" she asked more quietly in case the older woman was no longer asleep. "Won't she be suspicious?"

"We'll think of a good excuse," Gary agreed, noticing the time. "Right now, I have to go. I have a client to meet for lunch, but I wanted to make sure everything would be set for when I get home."

"It'll be set." Caroline nodded as she agreed. "We'll see you tonight." Hanging up the phone, she paused with her hand hanging on to the receiver for a long moment as she considered how easily their plan could come unraveled. After all, this wasn't a game, and if the men who trashed her apartment found them, innocent people could be hurt or killed.

Looking around the spotless kitchen she had given a good scouring, she sighed. Having spent most of her life looking out for herself, it wasn't like her to worry about what might happen to someone else. But Dakota was just a kid—a sweet and innocent child, and she would hate to see him pay in any way for her mistakes.

Keeping herself busy with lunch and more cleaning for the afternoon, Caroline tried to not think about what her hiding place could cost them. Shortly after four o'clock, she greeted the youngest member of the household at the front door. "How was school today?" she asked as she helped him out of his jacket.

"School," he repeated, tearing himself away and darting for his stash of toys.

"Hey, now!" she called after him, catching his arm and insisting he stop and speak to her. "You may play after our conversation." Working to garner his attention, she knelt before him and waited patiently until he had looked her in the eye. Then she repeated, "How was school today?" in a slow, well-enunciated style.

"School," he repeated, anger sending his voice up a few decibels.

"Yes." Caroline smiled warmly. "Say 'school was fine,' and I will let you go."

"School's fine," he managed with a bit of drool.

Catching the trickle of slobber with a napkin from her pocket, Caroline nodded encouragingly. "That's it, Dakota. Manners are important!" Once he had been cleaned and returned her grin in his crooked fashion, she released his arm, and he resumed course for the box in the corner.

"He's a handful," Lanelle informed her from the doorway, having taken up the location to watch the exchange.

"Yes," Caroline agreed. "Candy mentioned she would like to see his social behaviors improve. The impulsiveness I think we can curtail. Not sure what we can do about the spitting, though."

"It's part of his condition," the boy's grandmother explained.

"I know. I looked it up last night while I was in bed. He's better off than some but not as well off as others." Standing straighter, she announced, "Daks, you have one hour to play. Then dinner will be ready, and we will need to eat when Gary gets home." Eyeing Lanelle as she brushed past her, the blonde made for the kitchen to begin preparing the meal and to contemplate exactly what Mr. Ford might be thinking with his current course of action.

EIGHT

Any Day Now

CANDY HAD FELT odd about having Caroline Baker in her home from the moment Gary had suggested it. Therefore, walking in the back door that night to find her, Ben, and her family seated at dinner when she arrived home over an hour early hardly qualified as a surprise. Seeing the shocked expression on all of their faces confirmed any suspicions she had been unwilling to voice.

"Hey, more company!" Candice played it off with a smile. "I guess Ben is here to woo his secretary back to her desk?"

Latching on to the offered excuse, Gary joined in with a boisterous laugh. "I mentioned we had hired her, and he insisted on my arranging a meeting on neutral ground."

Serving her plate of steak and salad, Candy joined the group, noting that Caroline occupied her favorite chair next to Daks. Taking a seat beside her mother, who preferred sitting against the wall on the end next to her bedroom door, she watched as the new nanny seemed to have settled into her role with ease.

Eating and monitoring as Dakota munched on his carrot sticks, Caroline could feel the tension building in her shoulders and neck. She had known as soon as she hung up the phone with Gary that trying to sneak behind the woman of the house's back was a mistake —a lie that they had begun weaving the moment she had arrived there.

"Here, Daks." The young woman reached over to help her charge with his fingers on his fork. "That's it," she praised. She could almost feel the burn of Candy's squinted orbs as they glared at her, and regret stole what had remained of her appetite. Managing a few bites between helping the boy, she waited until most appeared to have completed the meal before she stood to clear the table.

Watching the blonde as she scraped plates and loaded the dishwasher, Candy wondered what the trio had really been up to. The situation had gnawed at her ever since she left the house that morning, and by the time class had ended for the evening break, she couldn't take it anymore. She had to know what was going on. She had skipped the lab in order to get home and check on things and settle the situation once and for all.

"Mom, are you going to give Dakota his bath tonight?" Candy asked sweetly.

"Yes, of course." The older woman smiled with obvious pleasure. "Caroline may be the new nanny and housekeeper, but bath time is still all mine."

Claiming the boy's hand, she led him into her private quarters and closed the door, where a tub full of bubbles would soon occupy them for at least half an hour.

Spying the satisfied smirk on his wife's face, Gary knew he was in trouble. Leaning back in his chair, he studied her soft features and waited for her to begin her assault. When she didn't speak, he offered, "They dismissed you early tonight?"

"No," she replied flatly, shaking her head slowly.

Running his hands over his stubble, Gary cut his eyes over at Ben, who had remained silent from the moment of her arrival. "Are you sick?" he tried again, hoping for an innocent reason for her busting in on them.

"No, Gary," she bit, her teeth grinding slightly.

"Maybe I should be going," Benjamin finally spoke up, getting to his feet.

Cutting her eyes over at him, they gleamed like sharp daggers when Candy rebuked him, "What's your part in this, Ben?"

"My part?" He scoffed, patting his chest with the tips of his fingers. "I'm not sure what you're talking about."

"The hell you don't," Candy hissed. "Yesterday, my husband shows up with your secretary in tow, insisting that we give her a job and a place to stay after she has left *your firm* for some mysterious reason. Then, twenty-four hours later, you're here, and the three of you are cozy as kittens, eating dinner with my mother and son while I'm supposed to be in class. Coincidence? I don't think so!" she practically shouted.

"Baby, calm down," Gary soothed.

"I am calm!" she screamed back. "I just want to know what the hell is going on here!"

Exchanging glances between the three of them, Caroline finally spoke up. "Candy, I'm really sorry about all of this. I didn't know who I could trust—"

"Who you could trust?" the other woman cut her off. "What is going on, Gary?" she addressed her mate through a clenched jaw.

"Could you two wait in my office for a moment? Candy and I need to talk for a minute, and then I'll be in and we can finish our business," Gary instructed calmly.

Dropping her cloth in the sink, Caroline ceased her cleanup and left the room with Ben close behind.

After the pair had disappeared down the hall, Gary swallowed hard and then began to confess, "Honey, I'm sorry we made you worry. That was not my intention."

"I'll bet," she shot back, causing his brow to furrow. "I don't understand why you would lie to me. Do you not trust me? Is there some secret you guys are in on, something you're planning or they're planning?"

"It's not like that," his voice cracked, hardly above a whisper. "Something's happened, Candy, something terrible, and I didn't want to get you involved."

"And bringing her into our home doesn't make

me involved?" Candy sniffed, her hands clenched into fists on the table in front of her.

Leaning towards her, Gary placed his fingers over hers. "I didn't want you to worry. I didn't think you would be in any danger. We would figure everything out, and it would all be fine."

Her eyes wide, she glared at him in dismay. "Why would I be in danger? What have you done?"

"I haven't done anything yet. Caroline came to me yesterday. She had some suspicions about a few fires that had taken place over the last couple of years. And since I had been an arson investigator, she thought I could help." He stared into her warm hazel eyes as he spoke, not daring to look away.

"And you were more than willing to help her out," Candy surmised.

"No. I wasn't. Not at first. But when she explained that the first fire was the one that destroyed your apartment two years ago…" His voice trailed away, and he shrugged. Swallowing, he felt foolish at having hid the truth from her. "I should have told you last night, but I wasn't sure what to make of it all."

"And how does Ben fit into the picture?" Her tone still roiled with angry undertones.

"He was here…last night. It wasn't someone from the office. He's the one who interrupted dinner. He had just made the same discoveries that Caroline had made, and he also thought of me as a source of help."

"Seems your good guy reputation is well known," she said with a slight grin at his discomfort. "Go on."

"Well, it is well known." He withdrew his grip on

her and leaned back in his chair. "You have no idea how hard this has been. I've never kept any secrets from you, and this one was about to tear me apart!"

Studying him for a long moment, Candy finally asked in a calmer voice, "So are they right?"

"I can't say for sure, but after having a look at the evidence today, I think we need to investigate further," he replied, glancing at the closed door of his mother-in-law's suite. "They'll be done soon. I think we should move to my office and finish this discussion away from innocent ears."

NINE

Priorities

STOMPING DOWN THE HALL, Candy couldn't wait to get Gary into his office and slammed the door behind her after they had entered. Her anger boiling red-hot through her veins, she intended to let all three of them have it but stopped cold when she realized that Caroline had been crying. "What are you blubbering about?" she demanded instead.

"Candy, I'm so sorry." The other woman sniffed while adjusting her grip on a wad of tissues. "I know we don't know each other very well, but your mother and son are both wonderful people. I'm sure that applies to you as well."

"And?" Candice snipped.

"And she needs our help," Gary stated firmly, closing the discussion. Opening his briefcase, he withdrew the envelope of evidence and unclasped the flap. Laying each of the stacks out on his desk, he continued, "I had a chance to go over these today, and

I agree that there are some oddities that bear further research, starting with the investigator of the fires."

"Harvey Waters," Ben interjected.

"Yes," Gary agreed, picturing his slender previous coworker.

"Harvey Waters," Candy echoed, recalling the guy from her few visits to Gary's office when he had been at the county investigator's department. "You know him." She glared at her mate.

"Yes." Gary smiled slightly. "Balding head, scrawny build, and smokes like a freight train. Pretty ordinary guy by all appearances."

"So, what does he have to do with this?" Caroline asked in a meek voice. "Did someone really set everything up, or is he simply incompetent?"

Gary and Ben exchanged glances, then Gary soothed, "I think it was intentional. If it had been a coincidence, no one would have needed to search your place, looking for whatever it is they think you've got. I'm still curious how they knew to go after you. Any idea how they knew, Caroline?"

Her crystal blue orbs staring back at him, the blonde swallowed her reply. She had a good idea why she had been targeted but still didn't understand how they had located her. Shifting her gaze, she watched the other woman while she formulated her response, then mumbled, "I'm not sure how they found out. Maybe someone I contacted about those documents just got suspicious."

Ignoring the exchange, Candy adjusted the pages on the desk with trembling fingers, noting her old address on the top of one of the stacks. Lifting it to flip through it, she shrugged. "What is all this stuff?"

"There's insurance documents, statements of record, and a copy of the official findings from the investigation, which Harvey signed. All four fit in a neat little package. Two fires two years ago, two fires last year. If there's been any this year, I haven't heard about them yet," Ben summed up the situation. "I filed the paperwork for the last of the claims a few weeks ago, and we finalized the details on it last week. It took the better part of a year for my client to get paid on this last one, but it finally went through. Of course, that's when I noticed that something didn't seem quite right about it, and I came to Gary for help."

Moving to the next stack, Candy continued her inspection, only half-hearing as Gary continued to question Caroline, who seemed to be evading him with her responses. Once she had viewed them all, she asked, "What are you going to do about this?"

"Well"—Gary inhaled deeply, and his voice deepened—"we're going to ask a few quiet questions and get a few answers. I've already put together a short list of people I think can and will help us. Harvey is the senior investigator here at the fire department. He's got respect, and he's got friends."

Ben shook his head slowly, examining the list of names Gary had produced. "I see you have Tom Harris on here. I've deposed him as a witness a couple of times. I think I could get him into the office without any suspicions being raised. But Christmas is in a couple of weeks, so we will have to act quickly before things start shutting down for the holiday."

Candy shivered at the mention of her least favorite time of year—the time where things seemed to always be the darkest for her.

"That'll be fine," Gary agreed. "I'll need to have a case of some kind as well—something I need to file and have you working on. We'll schedule the meetings around noon. You can send your new secretary to lunch, and we'll have the place to ourselves for our chat since our priority here is to find out everything we can without getting too many people involved."

His eyes flicking over at his wife, he noticed she had remained silent even though she appeared fully engrossed in their conversation. "Are you ok, baby?" he prodded.

"Yeah," she agreed, nodding slightly. "I just can't believe someone would burn a building on purpose, much less one with people still in it. Everyone made it out of our building, but people died in some of these fires!"

His spine tingling, Gary agreed, "I know. It's one of the reasons I loved my job. Helping people, if you know what I mean."

Studying his deep brown orbs, Candy knew exactly what he meant. Offering the slightest curl of her lips, she agreed, "Ok. You guys find out what you can, and I'll help if you need me."

"Ben and I will handle the investigating," Gary replied, standing up straighter and smoothing his pristine shirt. "You have finals next week, and I really want that to be your focus. Carol will take care of Mom and Daks." Glancing over at their new house-keeper, he could see the fire in her eyes and realized his mistake. "Sorry. *Caroline* will take care of things around here."

"Then I think things are settled," Ben agreed. "I'll set the meeting up for Tom on Thursday if I can, and I'll let you know what time to come in and confirm the date."

Her eyes darting between them, a glimmer of sadness washed over the petite young woman standing in their midst as she fully realized this Christmas could turn out to be the most terrifying she had ever experienced.

TEN

Ring the Bells

WHEN CLASS DISMISSED a few minutes before three on Friday afternoon, Candy leapt up from her seat and shoved her journal of notes into her backpack. If she hurried, she would catch the early bus and make it to the house before Daks got home.

"Candice, can I speak to you?" Professor Bryant caught her before she could get away.

Rolling her eyes, then removing her disdain from her features before she turned to face him, the young woman managed a pleasant tone. "Sure. What can I do for you?"

Watching as the majority of the class made a hasty exit, he held up a page covered in red marks. "I have some bad news," he said quietly, "but I'm willing to work with you on this if you can give it a redo this weekend."

Accepting her work and staring at the notations, she sighed. "I've really been trying, Dr. Bryant."

"I know you have, and you've made a great deal

of progress." He nodded as he spoke, free to use a normal tone as they had been left alone in the lecture hall. "Candice, you get an A for effort. That's why I'm giving you a second chance on this one. Give it a rework and drop it by my office on Monday. I'll consider it when I'm grading the final exam."

"Yes, sir," she replied through pursed lips. "But if I choose not to, how will it affect my grade in the class?"

"You'll probably end up with a D," he replied, tossing his pack over his shoulder and sidling towards the door. "You can do this, Candy. I have confidence in you. I can't wait to see your revisions."

"Ok." She sniffed, tucking the page in her own bag and zipping it up as he walked away at full stride. *Damn it*, she thought to herself as she pumped her short legs in quick steps, only to see the bus pull away from the stop well before she could get there.

It would be an hour before the next one came around, so she turned towards the library instead and spent the next thirty minutes working on the paper. She would have to study for her finals that weekend, so getting this new task out of the way before she went home was probably a good idea even if she hated not being there when Daks arrived at the house.

Shortly before five, Candy finally made it, trudging through short drifts of snow that had accumulated during the day. She had been thankful it had been light and not a repeat of the blizzard that had delayed her wedding last year. There might be a white Christmas ahead, but at least it would be a tame one.

Stomping her feet a few times on the back porch, she entered the kitchen and paused to enjoy the aroma of simmering stew. "Wow, that smells nice," she mumbled, lifting the lid and giving the giant pot a stir.

She could hear her son babbling in the other room and made her way to the door while removing her coat and scarf. Seated on the floor in the center of the giant rug, he pretended to drive his truck and put out an invisible fire. Beside him, Caroline positioned the police car and made siren noises before giggling contentedly.

"Here, Caro'," Dakota instructed, pointing out the desired location.

Moving the toy to obey his command, the blonde continued to smile, and the story unfolded for a few more minutes before Daks noticed his mother hovering over them. "Mom," he squealed, leaping to his feet to give her a hug. "Caro' fires truck." He beamed.

"I see." Candy laughed, happy he had enjoyed his afternoon. "Where's Mom?" she inquired, turning her attention to the blonde as she got to her feet.

"She went to lie down about three," Caroline informed her. "I'm afraid she might be coming down with something. I put on the stew, hoping something warm and filling might help." Her crystal blue orbs twinkled with concern.

Seeing her distress, Candy grew tense. Pushing the urge to rush into her mother's bedroom aside, she purposely slowed her movements as she placed her coat and other winter protection on her hooks at the back door. Then, stepping quietly, she entered her mother's space, noting the darkness of the room. Switching on a small lamp next to the bed, she felt her mother's cheek. *Burning up.* "Mom." She pushed at her gently, giving her a small shake. "Mom, I think you have a fever. Did you take anything for it?"

"No," Lanelle replied, stirring slightly but not making any real effort to get out of the bed. "I'm so tired."

"Let me get you something to drink and a few tablets. I think you're getting a cold, and you know how dangerous that can be," Candy stated firmly. Back in the kitchen, she located her mother's preferred cold remedy and punched a few of the gel tabs out of the foil pack.

"Is she ill?" Caroline inquired while giving the meal a stir and adjusting the burner a small amount.

"I think she's coming down with something, yes. She's susceptible to pneumonia, so we need to keep it under control. Otherwise, we'll be at the ER by Sunday," Candy replied. Filling a glass with water and a second with orange juice, she took them both and the medication in to her mother. "Here you go," she said cheerily, placing everything on the nightstand and helping her mother to sit up in her bed.

While she tended to the older woman, Gary arrived home and made his boisterous entrance. Candy smiled at Dakota's excited calls, then said softly, "Do you want to join us for dinner, Mom? Or should I bring a tray and sit in here with you?"

"I'll come out there," Lanelle agreed, having

taken the pills and finished off the glass of water. "Bring the juice, would you?" she asked as she got to her feet. Pulling the handmade blanket off the foot of the bed, she dragged it behind her as she crossed the threshold and took her favorite seat next to her door.

Setting the glass on the table before her, Candy dropped the blanket lovingly across her mother's shoulders. "I'll get you a bowl," she whispered, noting that Caroline had taken care of Daks and Gary had gone to wash up.

A few minutes later, everyone had been served, and spoons clinked as they enjoyed the delicious meal. "Well, I have to rewrite a paper this weekend. And I need to study for those finals next week," Candy announced between bites.

"I'm taking the weekend off," Gerald replied. "I'm sick of work," he tacked on with a chuckle.

"You two can rest up and study. I'll take care of the meals and keep an eye on Dakota," Caroline informed them with a full grin.

Candice nodded her approval. The other woman had obviously settled into her new role easily and even appeared to be enjoying herself, which was a good thing. Tom had been unable to make room in his schedule for their meeting as they had planned, so at the rate they were going, the young blonde might be hiding at their house for months before they could get things worked out and she would be free to return to her old life.

"I'll study tomorrow." Candy smiled, giving her mother's shoulder a pat. "Tonight, let's take it easy together. Ring the Christmas bells and enjoy each other's company for a few hours."

Lifting his glass in a mock toast, Gary agreed, "I'll put some music on when we've finished eating. And then we can decide if we want to light the fire."

"Oh, I would love a fire!" Caroline squealed, then flushed. "Sorry. I'm probably overstepping my bounds as *the help*."

"Nonsense," Gary chided, giving his wife a wink. "Candy loves the fire, and it looks like Lanelle could use it this evening," he observed, eyeing his mother-in-law's pale features. "We'll make a full evening of it. And stop thinking less of yourself. You're becoming a part of this family, Caroline."

Candy would have argued, but there would have been little point. Besides, the four days the other woman had been there, things had gotten a little easier on her with each one. If they didn't get rid of her soon, she would be completely spoiled and would probably be sad to see her go in the end.

ELEVEN

Dead of Winter

CANDY AWOKE EARLY SATURDAY MORNING, Gary still slumbering beside her in the darkness. Slipping from beneath the covers, she peeked out the window to find that it had snowed more overnight, and their back yard now lay covered in a thick blanket of white that sparkled in the dim light. *Damn. Another week before it had gotten bad would have been nice.*

Gathering her clothes as quietly as she could, she moved to the bathroom and closed the door before flicking on the light. Donning a warm sweater and jeans, she exited through the empty connected bedroom and made her way downstairs to start some coffee and get to work on her paper before she dug into her review for her final exams.

Noting her mother's door was closed, she turned on the light and began the task of filling the pot, only to be startled by the sound of a rasping cough on the other side of the wall. Pausing with the carafe suspended in midair over the device, she stopped her pouring to listen. Then, finishing the task, she pushed the button to begin the brew cycle.

Creeping into her mother's room, she whispered loudly, "Mom, are you awake?"

"Candy," her mother croaked back, sending chills through her entire body.

"Oh, God, Mom," Candy breathed, crossing the gap and dropping onto the unoccupied side of her mother's full-sized bed. Finding her hands clutching the blanket against her chest, the stiff digits felt frigid. Sliding off the bed and standing, she commanded, "Lay still. I'll get Gary, and we'll take you in."

"I'll be fine," her mother replied, her words slurred before she began to cough. Turning on her side, she curled into a ball as the spasm subsided. "Let me sleep," she mumbled, but Candy could no longer hear, having left the room, and stomped noisily up the stairs in her haste.

"Gary!" she called loudly as she flung open their door. "Baby, wake up! Mom has to see the doctor right now!"

Stretching and then rubbing his face, her husband prepared for the glare by covering his eyes. "Ok, hit the lights." The room blazed bright white when she flipped the switch and he could blink at her. "You think this is a hospital visit, or will the clinic suffice?"

"Hospital, definitely. She's coughing, and her hands are like ice," she informed him while she pulled out clothing for him to put on. "I'm sorry to ruin your sleeping in," she said more gently when she presented them to him.

"It's not your fault, hon," he replied, accepting the bundle. "I guess a shower is out of the question?"

Staring at him, she bit her lower lip, her heart racing. "Hurry, and I'll get her ready," she replied, turning to exit. Realizing Caroline would have to be informed, she stopped to knock lightly on the other woman's door. *At least we won't have to drag Dakota with us.*

A moment later, the wooden panel opened a crack, and Caroline asked through a yawn, "Yes? What's going on?"

"Mom's worse," Candy informed her. "We're going to take her down to the hospital. I assume you'll be ok with Daks while we're gone?"

"Yes, of course!" the other woman replied crisply, losing her tired demeanor in an instant. "Let me get dressed, and I'll be right down to help," she agreed while shutting the portal in Candy's face in her hurry.

Clomping down the stairs, Candy glanced at the fresh pot of coffee and poured a mug for herself, then one for her mother, and carried them into her mother's room. Placing the two on the nightstand, she leaned over to reach her and ran her hands firmly over her mother's back. "Mom, I brought you a cup of coffee."

Rolling over, the older woman allowed her to help her sit up, which produced a fit of coughs. Once they had subsided, she accepted the warm mug and wrapped her fingers around it. Holding the hot liquid in front of her face, she inhaled the warm steam it produced. "Thank you," she whispered.

Taking a seat in the corner chair on the other side of the nightstand, Candy lifted her own beverage and took a noisy sip. "Gary is getting a shower, and then we'll get you into the car for the trip."

"We should put blankets into the back seat for her," Caroline stated from the doorway, where she stood pulling her blond strands into a ponytail before she twisted them into a bun.

"That's a good idea," Candy replied, studying her for a long moment. "There's a linen closet upstairs with extra blankets stacked at the top."

"Ok. I'll get them," their nanny replied as she moved to comply.

Sitting together in the still of the morning, Candy's heart pounded heavily in her chest. Watching her mother as she sipped her coffee, she breathed deeply and tried to appear calm. She hated the dead of winter—the months when it was cold and snow covered the ground. *Nothing good ever happens to me at Christmas time,* she lamented, slapped immediately with the reality that it wasn't true.

Yes, her apartment had burned to the ground at Christmas. But Gary had saved her mother and son and had made sure they never lacked for anything since. *And last Christmas, we were married, despite the blizzard,* she recalled to herself.

Her mother lowered her cup as she delivered a few loud coughs, and Candy moved to sit beside her, placing her right arm firmly around the older woman's shoulders to steady her.

"I think these will work," Caroline called from the

door while holding up two quilts that Gary's great aunt had made.

"I don't know if he will want to use those," Candy replied, getting to her feet and relieving her mother of her mug. Carrying them into the kitchen, she poured both drinks into the sink and continued, "They're family heirlooms, but we'll see."

"What are they for?" Gary inquired as he joined the two women.

"To put in the back seat," Caroline replied, raising her chin slightly. "To make Lanelle more comfortable and keep her warm during the trip to the hospital."

Her thoughtfulness outweighed any remorse at using the pair of ancient blankets, and he smiled. "That's a great idea. I'll go pull it over as close to the house as I can and let it warm up inside before we take her out. Is she dressed?"

"Not yet," Candy replied. "Get the car warm, and I'll make sure she's ready when you are."

Fifteen minutes later, the trio helped the older woman out to the awaiting SUV, Gary and Candy each holding an arm to guide her and Caroline following with the blankets. Spreading one on the seat, the couple helped the older woman climb in and then covered her with the other. Closing the door with a firm thud, Gary gave the former secretary a nod. "We'll call you when we have some news."

"Don't worry," she replied with a hint of a smile. "I'm sure she'll be fine, and I'll take care of Daks while you're gone."

Climbing into the passenger seat, Candy

anxiously fastened her seatbelt as she watched Gary make his way around to the driver's side. Once he had them turned around and eased out the drive, they crept along over the frozen road. They had driven the path between the hospital and their home too many times to count since they had been together, and she wished like hell they could have gotten by this year without it.

TWELVE

Twists and Turns

CANDY SAT CURLED in the chair in her mother's room when Gary arrived home from work on Monday evening. At her feet sat a stack of books and a couple of journals of notes, and she had obviously dozed off while reading over a third. Removing the wirebound notebook from her limp fingers, he laid a blanket across her and let her sleep.

They had only kept Lanelle overnight at the hospital, and she had been home in her own bed by Sunday afternoon, giving Candy a few hours to finish her rewrite and cram for her exams. The hardest one had been earlier that day, and he hoped that she had done well enough to at least pass the course, for her sake.

Turning to the bed, he could see that Lanelle's clear blue eyes studied him as he fawned over his wife. "How do you feel?" he whispered, leaning closer so she could hear.

"Better," his mother-in-law replied, turning on her

back so he could sit on the edge of her bed. "You've been so good to us, Gary. Candy is so blessed to have you in her life. We all are."

Taking the seat, he clasped her small, frail hand with his and rebuked her gently, "Nonsense. You're my family, and I love you all." Standing, he leaned over and kissed her forehead. "Get some sleep, and we'll help you out to sit at the table for dinner if you like," he offered warmly.

"Yes, sir." She grinned up at him as he switched off the light and closed the door on his way out.

In the kitchen, Caroline stood over the stove, where she had been preparing their dinner for the oven.

"How long before we eat?" he asked as he washed his hands and dried them on a towel.

"About an hour," she replied with a smile. "Any news on my case?" she asked in return, hoping they had made at least some headway.

"I wasn't able to be there for the meeting," he informed her as they moved to the living room to watch Dakota play. "Tom was scheduled to meet with Ben at four, and Ben will call me tonight and give me the details."

"I hope he can do something for us. This is so nerve-racking, feeling like something could happen to me...or any of us, really, at any moment." She sighed as she took one end of the sofa beneath the front window.

Stoking the fire, Gary threw on a few more pieces of wood. "There's something else I've been meaning to ask you," he stated calmly as he took the chair that shared the end table next to her. "The other night, you said you weren't sure how they knew to come after you. But there had to have been something you did that gave yourself away. Someone you talked to who warned them that you were onto something."

Watching him adjust into his seat, Caroline felt sick. She had hoped she had gotten past that tidbit of poor judgment, but apparently, Gary wasn't going to let it slide. "I made a mistake," she finally admitted in a quiet voice. "I really didn't want to talk about it in front of Ben and Candy, either."

"So, what did you do, exactly? It's just us, and Daks isn't going to tell anyone." He chuckled, indicating the boy on the floor with an open palm.

"I know, Gary." She sighed, brushing at her leg as she tucked her feet beneath her. "It was stupid. I didn't think about the consequences when I did it—what it could cost me. As it turns out, it cost me everything." She sniffed, obviously disturbed by the realization.

"Just spit it out," he reassured. "But be quick before we get interrupted."

"I made a fake email account, and I sent Harvey Waters a demand for fifty thousand dollars," she said in a rush.

Her words sinking in, Gary's jaw dropped, and in his silence, she gushed on.

"I don't even see how they knew it came from me. I used a fake name to create a Gmail account and even sent it from the office instead of my home computer."

"When did you do this?" Gary managed, sitting forward in the chair, obviously disturbed by the news.

"About three months ago," she confessed. "I just sent it the one time and then logged in every once in a while to see what he replied, but he never did. As far as I know, he never even read the email."

"Well, obviously he read it," his voice grew louder. "He sent someone to search your place. Carol, you should have told us about this at the beginning! There can't be any doubt that Harvey did this!" Leaping to his feet, Gary fished his cell phone out of his pocket and made a call while heading to his office. Inside, he shut the door and listened to the ring before Ben's answering service picked up. "Sorry, wrong number," he clipped before he hung up.

Turning on his heel, he swung the door open to find Caroline standing in the hall. "I need Ben's cell number," he demanded loudly. "Now, Caroline!"

Not about to argue, she stepped past him and scratched it onto a notepad for him with a pen from the desk. "I'm sorry," she whispered as she handed it to him. "I was ashamed of what I had done. And I still don't see how he knew it came from me."

"The IP address," he dropped casually as he dialed and placed the device to his ear. "It wouldn't have been hard for him to trace it back to you with his skills and connections. You probably didn't even bother to use a different computer."

"I used the one at my desk," she admitted as her

face flushed. "Oh my God, Gary! Do you think they will do something to Ben?"

The man in question answered the call at that moment. "Hey! Wasn't expecting to hear from you tonight."

"Ben, we have a problem," Gary informed him without preamble. "If you're still at work, you need to get out of there and don't come here. I'll meet you at your place instead," he suggested while tapping the notepad as an indication for her to provide him with the address.

"I'm not at the office," Ben replied. "In fact, I'm only about two blocks away right now."

"You're coming here? Why would you come here?" Gary panted, struck by near panic.

"Relax. It's nothing like that. I've got great news, and I wanted to share it with you both at the same time." Ben laughed.

"Fine. We'll see you in just a minute," Gary snapped, ending the call abruptly.

"He'll be here any second," he informed the girl next to him. "He said everything was going to be fine, but with your latest bombshell, I'm scared to death at what might happen next," he growled as he pushed past her and headed for the back porch to await his arrival.

The crash came as a loud boom that seemed to roll through the air, tumbling over the houses and crushing Gary's family home under its weight. Frozen, staring at one another, the pair had stopped breathing as they waited, listening to the silence. Then suddenly, Gary leapt into action.

Spinning, he fled the office and double-checked the front and back doors, finding both to be secure. Then back in his office, his hands shook as he dug in his briefcase to retrieve the flash drive he had created storing all the documents they had put together on the case.

"What are you doing?" Caroline whined when she finally found her voice. "Was that Ben?" her voice cracked, and a tear rolled down her face.

"I can't say without going to look, and I can't leave you guys here alone," he informed her as his computer booted. "Right now, I need to drop this file in as many mailboxes as I can reach."

"What is that? And how is that going to help?"

"I scanned your evidence when I made my copy. I hid my copy with instructions how to find it in case anything happened. And I kept the digital copy in case I needed to share it with anyone else, which is exactly what I intend to do," he explained in a rush. "Please go watch out the window and yell out if you see ANYTHING or anyone set foot on this property."

"What about Candy?"

"Let her sleep. There's not a lot she can do except worry at this point, and I'd rather let her get her rest."

THIRTEEN

No excuses

LOOKING DOWN at the boy who played in the front room as she entered, tears dripped from Caroline's chin. Taking up the corner next to the front door, she peeked out of the curtain and watched the darkness outside. Finding it difficult to see, she cut off the overhead lamp and said aloud, "Let's play in the dark, Daks."

With the small amount of light coming from the kitchen, he ignored her and simply gravitated in that direction with his play. Returning her attention to the window, her throat clamped shut as she let out a low squeal.

Dashing back to Gary's office, she managed through heavy breaths, "A black van just turned into the driveway. They have their headlights off."

"Ok. I'll meet them at the back," he agreed, opening the closet and then his gun safe that he kept hidden inside it. Removing a shotgun, he filled it with shells and then added a clip to his .9-mm pistol.

Carrying them both, he instructed, "Take Daks and go in Lanelle's room. Shut, lock, and barricade the door, and then call the police. Tell them we have a home intruder and to send help."

"What are you going to do?"

"I'm going to stall them and try to bargain for our lives," he replied, his features frozen in focused purpose as he made the turn into the kitchen and clomped towards the back door.

Behind him, Caroline dropped to her knees beside the boy. Taking hold of the bulky fire engine, she suggested, "Come on, Daks. Let's go play in Mimi's room."

Looking up at her with wide eyes, his simple understanding of the household rules intervened, and he failed to move. Unable to articulate, he simply replied, "Mimi's no."

"Tonight, Mimi's is yes," she encouraged, pulling his hand to guide him. "Come on. I'm bringing the woo-woos, and we can play with Mimi and Mommy."

Following reluctantly, the police car in his other hand, Caroline got him inside and closed the door, hearing the back door open as she leaned against it to lock it.

"What's going on?" Candy demanded in the darkness before switching on the lamp next to the bed.

Her mouth dry, Caroline could hardly form the words. "Something's happened. They've found us... found me. And Gary has gone out to confront them. He told me to bring Dakota in here with us and lock the door. We're supposed to block it up with every-thing we can find and call the police."

"Oh, sweet Jesus." Candy panted, grabbing her forehead and then using the hand to pull her hair back and grasp it into a knot on top of her head. Her mouth hanging open, she managed, "We have Mom's emer-gency call alarm. I don't have my cell. Do you have yours?"

Shaking her head, Caroline asked in a shaky voice, "Why is there no phone in this room?"

"Because it's on the wall right outside the door," Candy grunted back, stepping into the bathroom and yanking the cord on the wall between the tub and toilet. "This will notify the call center that there's an emergency."

"How do they respond?" Caroline asked, already pushing the large stuffed chair from the corner across to put in front of the door. The phone on the other side began to ring.

"They call," Candy replied, taking an arm and helping her position the back against the flat surface. "When no one answers, they'll try a few other numbers and then send an ambulance."

"Great," Caroline muttered. "They should get here in time to collect the bodies."

Gary waited until Caroline had entered Lanelle's small quarters and shut the door. Then, he cut off the kitchen lights and slowly cracked the back door. In the parking area sat a plain, black cargo van, it's engine still making quiet popping noises after having been recently driven.

He called, "We need to talk," into the darkness before he stomped out onto the porch, brandishing his weapons openly. "Who's out here?" he tried again. He could hear the boards creek on the far end of the veranda and turned slowly to find three men in a small huddle, apparently planning their next move.

"Is that you, Harvey?" Gary raised his shotgun and pointed it at the slender man, the obvious leader of the trio. "Come on closer," he commanded. "This is over...whether you like it or not. Hurting anyone else isn't going to change the outcome for you and your buddies here."

"No?" Harvey replied, taking a few slow steps in his direction. "I think we have the situation contained, as soon as we get inside."

"Wrong," Gary clipped. "I sent a digital copy of Carol's evidence to everyone in my friend's list, including everyone I knew when I worked for the county. I also told them about her attempt to black-mail you and where to find that evidence," he bluffed, but only to a small degree. "Hurting my family won't save you," he said more quietly.

In the distance, a siren drifted faintly on the air, and they all paused to listen. "You hear that? The police are already on their way," Gary grunted, adjusting his grip on his weapon.

"That's for the crash," Harvey informed him. "Putting old Benjamin in the ditch wasn't hard with the roads iced over the way they were today." He took another step closer, and Gary could see his fearless face; the man wasn't giving up.

"That's far enough," Gary spat, hoping to stall as long as possible before he shot the three of them down. "I need to know why you did this, Harvey. You were an investigator. It was your job to bring people to justice, not put them in danger. Do you know how many people died because of what you did?"

"Yeah, I know." Harvey grinned, causing Gary's stomach to turn. "But you had the same job. You know how thankless it is. How empty and meaningless, with pitiful pay, long hours, and dangerous conditions."

Gary would have interrupted to disagree, but he had the man talking and didn't want to shut him down, so he agreed instead. "Yeah, I know. Is that your excuse?"

"I don't need any excuses." Harvey chuckled. "I've been building a nice little nest egg for myself these last few years, and soon I'll be able to retire. I'll get out of this business just the way you did."

More sirens joined the song in the night air, moving closer.

"I have better pay," Gary informed him, "but it's not a better job. If you made all that money, why didn't you just pay her off and get away?"

"I had to shut her up." Harvey took another step

forward. "I had to be sure what she knew. I'm old enough to draw retirement next year. With the fires this season, I would have been set."

"This season?" Gary raised his brow in doubt.

"Yeah, winter. Christmas. Lots of fires happen around Christmas, Gary." Harvey sneered. "Dry trees, space heaters, fireplaces." He laughed. "Lots of innocent reasons that a building could go up."

"So, you burn them down and make it look like an accident. Do you set the fires, or do you just write them off?"

"I think I've shared enough," Harvey replied curtly, crossing the short distance between them as he reached for the gun.

Gary anticipated the move and dropped the weapon to the side, shooting the man behind Harvey in the leg.

Raising the pistol, he caught the man in front of him in the gut. "I said don't move!" he shouted, pointing both weapons at the only man left standing as the other two writhed around on the wooden surface in pain, the sirens louder than ever.

Raising his hands slowly, the final hoodlum looked around, as if considering which direction to run, when swirling blue and red lights flooded the yard, and a man leapt out of the ambulance as it came to a stop. "What's the emergency?" he called out.

"Hey, Bill," Gary replied, overwhelmed with joyous relief. "These guys thought it would be a good night for a little B and E with a side of arson. I guess they were wrong."

On the porch, the two EMTs assessed the gunshot wounds while Gary kept the third firmly in his sights. "Don't even try it," he hissed. "I'd shoot you before you even made it to the fence."

FOURTEEN

Eve Advice

"SURPRISE!" Eveline called as she entered her son's home. It was Christmas Eve, and they had arrived in town that morning to surprise their son and his family with gifts and holiday dinner.

"What are you doing here!" Candy squealed, throwing her arms around the taller woman for a hug. Realizing the awkwardness in her mother-in-law's stiff form, she released her and settled for a less enthusiastic half-squeeze from Roger. "Did Gary know you were coming?"

"No, silly girl. That's why it's a surprise," Eve informed her while removing her coat. Looking around, she wrinkled her nose and demanded, "Where is Gerald? It's Christmas Eve. Don't tell me he's working!"

"He's…" Candy hesitated. "He's at the hospital with Caroline and Ben. I think they are going to release Ben today, and they are going to help him get home and settled."

"That Gary." Roger shook his head with a chuckle. "He's always been the natural hero in every situation."

"Yes," Candy agreed. "I'm beginning to think he is addicted to saving people," she added quietly as she accepted their coats and placed them in the closet in the hall. "Are you staying for dinner?"

Eve could see the strain on her son's bride's features. "This is your wedding anniversary, Candice. You don't have any special plans?"

Leading them into the kitchen, Candy glanced into her mother's room, where Daks and Lanelle both lay sleeping, stretched out side by side on her bed. "Things have been hard this year, Eveline." She sighed, pouring herself a cup of warm coffee. "What am I saying? Things are hard every year. Christmas hates me."

"Christmas doesn't hate you." Eve smirked, preparing a cup for herself. "Gary told me about the incident with Caroline. I was furious that he put the three of you in danger to help her."

"I was, too," Candy agreed, turning to find Dakota standing in the doorway and rubbing his eyes. "Aww, honey, did we wake you?"

"How about I take him outside for a bit of snowman building," Roger offered, already retrieving his coat. "That way you girls can talk."

Helping her son into his winter gear, Candy silently agreed. She would hate to admit it out loud, but at the moment, she was in need of some great Eve advice. Closing the door once they were gone, she began in earnest, "I was so angry when Gary brought her home. But it was so incredible having her here, Eve. I mean, the cops and the guys who showed up to burn our house down weren't great, but Caroline herself was pretty fantastic. She cooked. She cleaned," Candy lamented as she curled into her mother's favorite chair at the table. "She took care of my mother and my son with nothing but love. How do we replace her?"

"Are you sure she's going to quit?" The older woman calmly sipped her brew, seated in the chair across from her.

"Yeah, I'm sure she will. Ben is going to give her back her job. She was a great secretary from all accounts." Candy sniffed. "Why would she choose being 'the help' over that? I mean, what can I do about it?"

"You should speak to her, Candice. Let her know that you want her to stay and be a part of your family if that's truly what you desire."

Candy glared at her. "You know what she did to Gary," she bit curtly. "I was thinking you would talk me out of this nonsense and convince me that her leaving was the best thing that could happen to us."

"I'm not going to convince you of anything." Eveline's laughter tinkled lightly. "Yes, I am aware of the circumstances between Caroline and Gary. She was a young and foolish girl, and I knew from the moment that I met her that she was lying about her pregnancy. I've never put much faith in the girls that Gary chose to date." She raised her coffee cup to the one who won her son's heart in the end. "Thankfully, I wasn't always right about them."

"You've got that right," Candy agreed with a tiny grin. "But she also tried to extort money from a criminal, and that wasn't so long ago. Who knows what she might do, living here in this house with us. Are you saying you would ask her to stay if you were in my shoes?"

Eve shrugged. "I can't say what I would do. I'm not in your shoes." She glanced around at the spotless kitchen. "What I can say is that I've never seen this house look better, and that includes when its previous owner occupied it. Even Aunt Betty couldn't keep it this spotless. I think Gary was right. You need someone to help out around here with the housework and with caring for Dakota and Lanelle. If that person is Caroline, then so be it."

Blinking at the older woman a few times, Candy allowed the words to sink in before she replied, "You have such a way with people, Eve. Every time I think you are going to react one way, you totally surprise me."

"Well, that's what I'm here for." She laughed in reply. "Now, how about we start dinner so everything is ready when Gary and Caroline get home."

FIFTEEN

Come and Go

CAROLINE RODE in the front seat of Gary's SUV, picking at her fingers anxiously. "What am I going to say to her? I've made such a mess of things. I should go back to my apartment and my old life and forget all about any of this."

"You could do that," Gary agreed, fairly certain that's not what the young woman next to him really wanted to do.

"Yeah, I could do that." She sighed.

Making the turn into his private drive, Gary's heart leapt into overdrive at the sight of his parents' car parked behind his house. "Damn," he muttered under his breath. "Mom and Dad are here."

"Your mom and dad?" She gasped. "Oh, no!"

"Relax. They already know what happened. I phoned and filled them in after everything had been taken care of with Harvey and his accomplices. We go in, and we act normal, and you don't have to explain anything."

"I'm not sure I can do this, Gary. I think I should go. Really."

"Then go up and pack your things, and I'll take you home," he pacified. He couldn't make her stay even if Candy still needed her. This was something the two women would have to work out between them, and he fully intended to stay out of it.

Parked in the garage, Gary climbed out and locked the vehicle when Caroline had exited the other side. Walking beside her, she seemed to move at a snail's pace. "Oh, look! They're building a snow-man!" he observed, indicating his father and stepson. "I think I'll go help, and you can take care of things inside."

"I thought you were taking me home!" she stated loudly.

"I will. Go get your stuff, and we'll go when you get back down," he called as he plowed through the deeper drifts, towards the work in progress. "Hi, guys! Need a hand?"

Watching him go, Caroline could feel the angry flush on her cheeks. *Just great. He left me to face his wife and mother alone,* the two people she felt had more reason than anyone to hate her at the moment.

Entering through the back door, she found the women seated at the table, along with Lanelle. The group fell silent as soon as she stepped inside. "Hello," she said politely, removing her jacket and hanging it on a hook. "I'm here to gather my things, and then Gary is taking me home." She walked stiffly past them, wiping at an escaped tear as she turned the corner and clomped up the stairs.

"She's leaving?" Lanelle stated in shock, still not fully understanding what all had taken place over the few weeks that the girl had been a part of their household.

Staring at her mother-in-law, Candy sighed heavily, who only gave her an exaggerated shrug before she said quietly, "Maybe you should go talk to her, Candy dear. Be sure everyone will be happy with that decision."

Biting her bottom lip, Candice followed the blonde calmly, then knocked quietly when she arrived in front of the closed portal.

"Who is it?" Caroline called from the other side.

"You know who it is." Candy giggled. "It's me." Grasping the handle, she opened the door a crack and asked, "Do you mind if I come in?"

"Not at all." The other girl sniffed, doing her best to hide her sorrow.

Closing the wooden panel behind her gently, Candy inhaled deeply and let the breath out nice and slow before facing her employee. "Caroline, I know I made a big deal when Gary brought you here," she began.

"Under false pretenses," Caroline filled in. "Don't forget that part." She had begun stuffing clothes into her suitcase but stopped as her shoulders shook. Crying, she sobbed, "I'm so sorry, Candy. I never meant to put any of you in danger."

"Hey," Candy shot back, taking the girl's arm and pulling her to face her. About six inches shorter, she looked up at the tall blonde and smiled. "I can't believe you're crying over this! We are fine. No one was hurt. The bad guys are in jail or will be once they get out of the hospital." She laughed.

"Stop it." Caroline pulled her arm away. "You guys would have had a great Christmas without me around to ruin it for you," she challenged.

"Christmas is tomorrow, silly," Candy reminded her.

"Yes, I know. Today is Christmas Eve. Oh my God, and it's your anniversary. I'll get a cab home, and you can have Gary for the rest of the day," she offered, returning to her packing.

"Is that really what you want?" Candy pushed the issue. "You don't seem very happy about it."

"I just don't think you guys will want me here after all I've done," she blubbered, her words slurred and unclear.

"After all you've done? Scrubbed every floor and flat surface in this house. Cleaned the carpets, the tubs, the toilets…the drapes. Oh, and taken excellent care of my mother and my son—neither of which is a small task."

She had never in her life wished she had been taller than she did at that moment. Reaching up, she brushed the hair out of the other girl's face, then laughed as her own tears spilled over onto her cheeks. "Crazy Caroline, don't you know? I never would have made it out of this semester if it hadn't been for you!"

"You don't mean that." Caroline pushed her hair behind her ear and faced her new friend fully. "I really didn't do much."

Shaking her head, Candy wrapped her in her arms the best she could. Fortunately, Caroline didn't fight her and accepted the hug graciously, then asked, "Are you sure you want me to stay here?"

"Only if you want to." Candy beamed. "Gary says we can afford to keep you on, and I really do appreciate all the help. Honestly, I think I would be doing at least one or two classes over if you hadn't been here to help get me through finals."

"And nearly get you—"

"Shh," Candy interrupted her. "I told you. We're fine. And all that wasn't your fault...exactly. I'm glad they were caught, and the guys who burned our apartment won't be doing that to anyone else, so thank you. And please, stay and be our nanny."

The corner of her mouth twitching, Caroline could feel her heart flutter. "You know, Candy. I don't have much family to speak of, and I don't have many in the way of friends either. But if I ever had a little sister, I think you might be what it would be like."

"Does that mean I can call you Carol?" The shorter girl giggled. "I've noticed that Daks does."

"Yeah, he does, but he can't say the rest." Biting her lip, she could feel her tears ready to make another appearance. "Ok, you sold me. You can call me Carol. A friend of mine once told me that nicknames are a show of affection."

"Yes, they are," Candy agreed, giving her another

squeeze, then inching towards the door. "I'll let you put all your stuff back in the drawers, and we'll see you in a few minutes so we can have dinner."

"Oh, right!" Carol nodded, her smile wide. "I'll be right down," she agreed as the door clicked closed.

SIXTEEN

Came and Went

OUTSIDE, Gary had joined in the snowman building but quickly found himself lost in thought with his father standing beside him. Across the yard, Daks seemed to be having the time of his life, rolling a crooked ball of snow and attempting to get it to grow into a proper mid-section for his creation.

"Dad, I really need to talk," he finally confessed.

"Are you unsure about keeping Caroline on as your housekeeper?" Roger inquired calmly, leading the way over to help his grandson free his lump of snow from being stuck.

"Actually, no. I'm pretty confident about that choice. I'm more in doubt about my position in the company. I'm not sure sales is the right place for me," he stated with a huff. "In fact, I'm not sure being in an office is the place for me."

Roger stood up straight and looked him in the eye. "Does Candy know about this?"

"I don't think so," Gary breathed, exhaling a thick

cloud of steam. "I've been pretending everything is fine for months now. I'm a little afraid to tell her. I really want to keep my word to her, but I have to admit it felt pretty darn good helping Carol out with her problem, and making sure those guys have their day in court will be fantastic."

"I see." His father nodded.

Gary could feel the doubt in his gut. He loved Candy more than anything, and the last thing he wanted to do was to let her down. Ice that cake with the fact his mother would be disappointed and it was more than he could bear. "Mother isn't going to like it," he stated more calmly. "She's wanted me there forever."

"Your mother will understand," Roger replied calmly, lifting the large ball into position and helping Daks start another for the head. "You have to do what makes you happy, son. You're going to be working another thirty or forty years. You don't want to spend all that time in a job you hate. If your time with the company came and went, then it's time to move on. End of story."

Nodding his understanding, Gary grinned. "Thanks, Dad." Leaving them to their assembly, he marched towards the house and knocked the snow off his boots before he went inside. "Hi, ladies," he greeted the two grandmothers warmly. "Where are Candy and Caroline?"

"Upstairs," Eveline informed him. "Girl talk. You probably shouldn't interfere."

"Probably not," Gary agreed, ambling into the

living room to wait. When his wife finally came down the stairs, he felt relieved that she was alone. "Has she decided to stay, or will I need to take her home?" he inquired after stealing a brief kiss. Using a hand on the small of her back, he guided Candy towards his office and closed the door so they could speak alone.

"She's staying," his bride replied, unable to hide her obvious joy at the decision. "I'm so glad she's going to be here, Gary. Thank you so much for bringing her into our lives," she cooed, then held up her hand to prevent him from making a reply. "But there's one thing I need to ask you to do."

"Anything, baby." He grinned, longing to sweep her into his arms and thinking he should save his request for another time.

"I think you need to go back to work for the fire department," she stated calmly.

Gary felt as if the wind had been knocked out of him. "You want me to do what?" he gasped.

"I want you to be happy," she answered calmly, swishing from side to side as she spoke. "I know how much you loved being at the firehouse and saving people's lives, Gerald Ford. We do what we are, and you are a rescuer. I can't change that about you. I love that about you. But please, don't ever bring anyone else home again. Not without asking me first."

"It's a deal," he squealed, stepping forward and pulling her off her feet and into his arms. "Oh my God. I thought you were going to be so angry! I never dreamed you would understand."

Hugging him tightly, she could feel her heart

pounding. "I didn't make this decision lightly," she replied against his chest. She still had her fear that she would one day get that call that meant he would never come home again, but it was a risk she felt she had to take. "I'm still scared of losing you," she reminded him as he set her back on her feet. "But I'm more afraid of not letting you be the man you were meant to be, and I could never live with myself if I took that away from you. Now, let's go get dinner made and celebrate year number one, Mr. Ford."

"After you, Mrs. Ford." He laughed, shutting off the light as he followed her out of the room.

Thank You

Thank you for reading, and I hope that you have enjoyed the 2017 installment of the Sweet Christmas Series. Look for a new adventure for Gary and Candy at Christmas next year. ~ Sam

Books in this series include:
    Christmas Candy (2015)
    Christmas Eve (2016)
    Christmas Carol (2017)
    Christmas Joy (2018)
    Christmas Holly (2019)
    Christmas Lane (2020)

About the Author

Anyone who knows me could tell you, I am a friendly kind of person, never met a stranger and take up conversations anywhere at any time. I work hard, and my mind never seems to shut down, as I wake up often in the middle of the night with ideas pouring out and demanding to be dealt with. Of course that means much of my books were written in the middle of the night.

I grew up and still live in the great state of Texas where everything is bigger, where we have warm weather and a central location. I love my state, my town, and my family, which includes my four sons, my significant other, and many friends as well.

I have thoroughly enjoyed writing this story and hope that you will love reading it just as much. And of course, there will be many more adventures to come.

You can follow Samantha Jacobey at:
Website: www.SamJacobey.com
Facebook: https://www.facebook.com/SamJacobey
Twitter: https://twitter.com/SamJacobey
Pinterest: http://www.pinterest.com/samanthajacobey/

Also by SAMANTHA JACOBEY

http://www.amazon.com/-/e/B00GEB5LX0

A New Life Series – an epic adventure, TORI FARRELL's life IS one wild story... escaped from a biker gang and running from drug lords... used by the FBI and hoping to protect her present from her past... IT'S DARK - IT'S BRUTAL, and it's WORTH EVERY MINUTE OF IT!! (Mature read, 18+ for graphic sexual content and violence, including rape)

Summer Spirit Novella Series - no one EVER had a summer romance like this... Charlie visits another plane, parallel to our own, where Summer Angels and Dark Angels battle over the fate of man. A unique twist on an old idea that will keep you guessing; will Charlie and Clarisse ever find their HEA? (New adult)

Teach Me to Prey – in this standalone thriller, JASON TRUITT and his friends have gotten their way for years. Deceit, sex, and foul play aren't normally covered in the curriculum, but they're doing whatever it takes to get under BECKY STEWART's skin. When one of the boys turns up dead, it's a race against time to save the others; a STUNNING STORY that will get your heart racing and leave you breathless by the end... (New Adult)

The Binding (Unexpected Magic #1) - One cursed diary will change two strangers forever...Can Meri and Rider use her mother's old book to figure out why someone is after them? Or will the guilty party succeed, ripping the tome away before killing them and then slithering back into the darkness… (New Adult)

The Wicked Awakened (Unexpected Magic #2) – a Halloween novel; a five-hundred-year-old witch wants to turn SARAH MATTHEWS' body into her new home… A twisted tale involving a coven hell bent on seeing that she succeeds. Who will come out on top in this epic battle of wills? (Mature read, 18+ for graphic sexual content and violence)

The Irrevocable Series - From affluent beginnings, BAILEY DEWITT's life has become a broken mess... after her parents died unexpectedly, she didn't think it could get any worse. But when the arrogance of man catches up and puts the entire world into a dooms-day spiral, there will be only ONE PLACE she can run to - the ONE PLACE she wanted desperately to escape. (New Adult)

The Dragon of Eriden Series - Amicia Spicer led a simple life, until she discovered it had all been a lie… On her deathbed, Arely Spicer confessed to her only daughter that she had been found by, not born to her mother and father. Sad news to be certain, the idea of having a family of flesh and blood waiting to be reunited sent the young, independent woman on the adventure of a lifetime. Little did she know, a dragon's heart beat within her chest and her journey would be more perilous than she could have imagined... (New Adult)

Also from our Lavish family

Love on the Double Duo
By L.A. Remenicky
http://mybook.to/LoveOnTheDoubleDuo

The Monroe brothers fall fast, they fall hard, and they fall forever. But the road to true love isn't always easy.

Loving Jessie's Girl – Book 1: Until AJ Monroe left Indiana after college he had always lived in his identical twin brother's shadow. He had made a life for himself in Denver, Colorado, away from Jessie, away from Indiana. But when AJ feared for his brother's safety, he left everything behind to step back into the shadow he thought he had outgrown. Finding his brother was AJ's only concern...until he met Jessie's girl.

Fiercely independent, Rina Abbot hid her true situation from everyone, including her best friend, Jessie. Out of money and unable to care for her rescue dogs she had no choice but to accept the help of the handsome stranger with a familiar face. Afraid to trust him, she tried to ignore the feelings he stirred within her as they searched for his missing brother.

But secrets never stay secrets for long.

Finally open about their feelings for each other, Rina's secrets began to wreak havoc on their lives. Would Rina's secrets force AJ to give up his dream of loving Jessie's girl?

Beyond Duty – Book 2: After serving in the Marine Corps, Jessie Monroe has finally found a life beyond war. He's focused on
  being an EMT and helping his best friend rescue dogs, until he happens upon a curvy blonde stranded
  with a flat tire and no jack.

On the run from her past, Dori Graham is slow to trust any man, and she tries to ignore the spark of
  interest she feels for her handsome savior, but a friendship grows between them.

When Dori's past invades her new life, Jessie vows to rescue her. Saving her will take him beyond duty
  and into his own personal hell. Calling upon his training as a Marine and the depth of his feelings for

Dori, Jessie will need the mental strength to battle to save her and, ultimately, save himself.

Between the Trees
Kathy Moczerniak
http://mybook.to/betweenthetrees

A beautiful coming of age with a dark side that one teenager must fight to overcome…

Beyond Kathryn Lucas' first memory of her father's tree lay a dysfunctional path of violence, heartbreak, and secrets within a family severely entrenched in the vicious cycle of abuse. A lifetime of fear drives her from her home, and the teenage girl finds refuge with an aunt and uncle determined to protect their niece.

Distressing flashbacks unravel in Kathryn's fragile mind among the turmoil encircling her as she struggles through adolescence and descends into her pain-ridden past. When the summation of her unsettling memories allows the darkness to overtake her, she becomes desperate to unearth the light.

Inspired by a true story, Kathryn must hold on tightly to those who love her, searching for her place in a world threatening to break her as she fights to overcome life's betrayals before she is deprived of her future.

The Hunter Series
Sara J. Bernhardt
http://mybook.to/HuntersTril

Jane Callahan is a reclusive, seventeen-year-old high school student dealing with the death of her beloved brother. Her home in Southern California with her mother is a constant reminder of her loss and pain. In hopes of escaping her past she moves to North Bend Oregon to live with her father, where she meets a beautiful boy named Aidan Summers.

Jane is intrigued by his looks as well as his unusual ways of attempting to get her attention. After months of uncommon conversation and frustration, an uncertain romance brews between Jane and Aidan, but Aidan has a ghastly secret that could destroy everything.